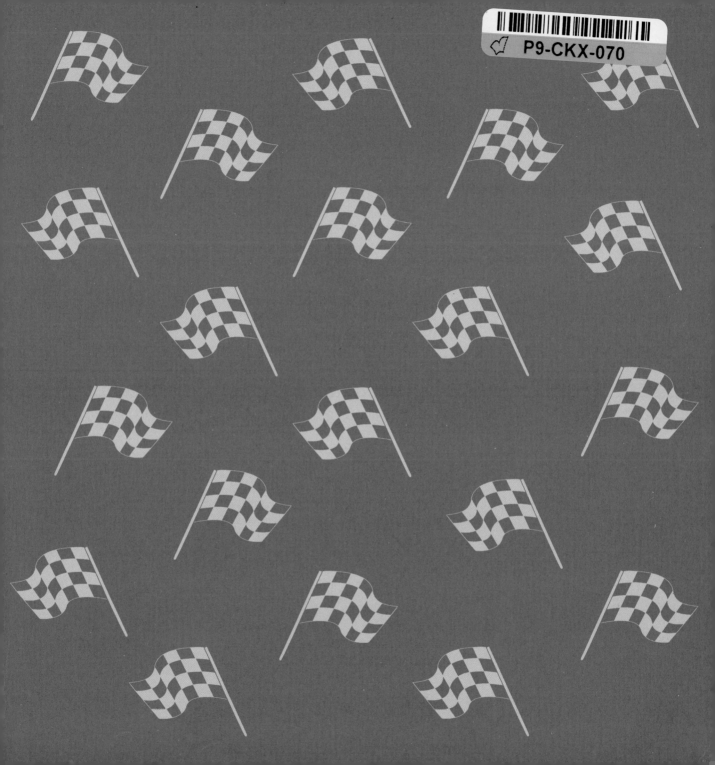

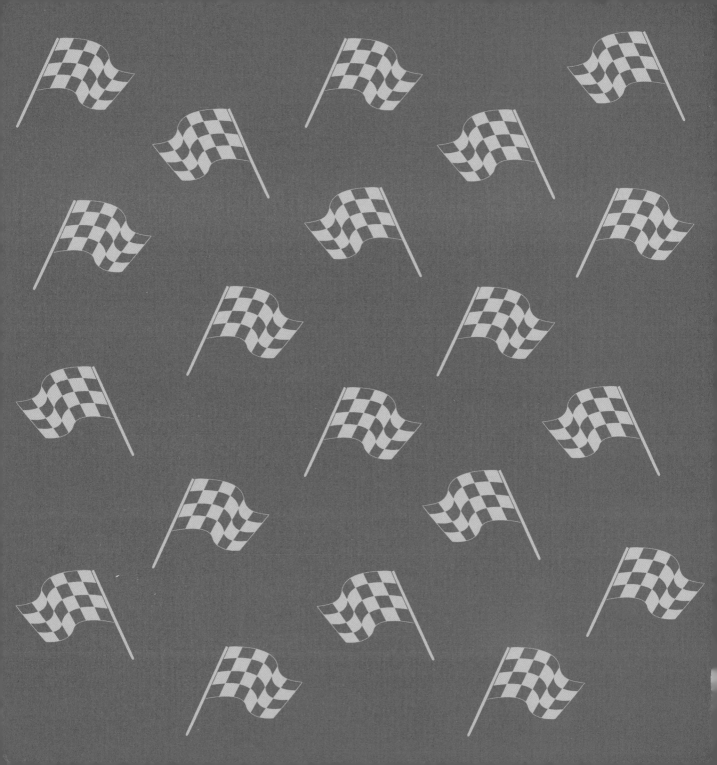

# Curious George®

## Boxcar Derby

**Adaptation by C. A. Krones**
**Based on the TV series teleplay written by Chuck Tately and Raye Lankford**

Houghton Mifflin Harcourt
Boston   New York

For information about permission to reproduce selections from this book, write to Permissions, Houghton Mifflin Harcourt
Publishing Company, 215 Park Avenue South, New York, New York 10003.

ISBN: 978-0-544-38078-3 paper over board
ISBN: 978-0-544-38077-6 paperback
Design by Afsoon Razavi
www.hmhco.com
Printed in China
SCP 10 9 8 7 6 5 4 3 2 1
4500558201

George loved cars. He loved riding in cars, washing cars, and playing with toy cars, too! George and Allie liked to race them on his toy racetrack.

They were outside playing when Bill rode by on his bicycle.
"If you like cars, you should come watch me race today on Boysenberry Hill!"
Bill said. He showed the man with the yellow hat a newspaper ad about the
boxcar derby that afternoon. George was curious.

The man spotted Bill's boxcar next door.
"Wow, Bill! Did you build that all on your own?"
"I sure did—all by myself!" said Bill.
That gave George and Allie an idea.

"You kids want to enter the derby?" the man asked. Of course they did! "I could help you build your car," he offered.

"Sorry, but that's against the rules," Bill interrupted. "Racers have to build their own cars."

Bill gave Allie and George the rulebook. It included everything they needed to know about the derby and building their very own boxcar.

"The race starts this afternoon at two o'clock sharp," Bill told them.
"You two better get to work," the man said. "Feel free to borrow anything
you see around the house. And good luck!"

George and Allie looked at the rulebook. Luckily, it had lots of pictures. The first thing they would need is the part to sit in—the body. Plus a steering wheel, wheels, and a brake. Now it was time to look around for car parts.

George borrowed the man's blue wagon—they could use that to carry car parts. They would have to hurry. The race was starting in two hours!

George and Allie walked past the Quints' house. Mrs. Quint was outside planting.
"We're building a boxcar to enter in the derby," Allie told her.
"Well, help yourself to anything you might see in my yard," Mrs. Quint said,
before going inside.

When George and Allie saw the old kayak in her yard, they had the same idea.
It would be perfect for the body of their car!
"It already has two seats in it, too—one for you and one for me," said Allie.
They were off to a great start.

Their next stop was Grandpa Renkins's barn. It was filled with all kinds of old parts they could use—especially wheels!
George found four that matched and nailed them to the kayak. They were ready to roll!

But something wasn't right. The wheels didn't roll! George remembered the picture in the book. Wheels turn on an axel—a rod that goes through the center of the wheel so it can spin.

The wagon's wheels were on axels! George and Allie nailed the kayak onto the wagon. They also used the wagon handle as a steering wheel. The car was almost ready. They just needed to find one more part—a brake.

Grandpa Renkins rolled up in his buggy. "Hey, kids! The race starts in ten minutes—are you ready?"

"Oh, no!" cried Allie. "We're still missing a part."

"Borrow anything you need," Mr. Renkins said, and parked his buggy.

"Oops. Almost forgot to put my brake on," he added.
Did he say "brake"? George and Allie took the brake off of Mr. Renkins's buggy and put it on their car. It was finally finished! They were going to make it just in time for the race!

"Hey—you made it!" said Bill, just as they were pulling up to the start line of the race. Their brake worked perfectly! Without a second to spare, Mr. Quint waved the flag and yelled: "On your mark, get set, go!"

They were off! George and Allie were neck and neck with Bill. It was a very close race.

George and Allie leaned forward and took the lead! That is, until Mr. Renkins's buggy came racing down the hill!
"Hey, what happened to my brake?" Mr. Renkins shouted. He chased after his buggy as it zoomed past George and Allie.

**Mr. Renkins jumped on the buggy just in time to cross the finish line in first place!**

George and Allie were runners-up. But with such a great boxcar, they felt like winners, too.

# Let It Roll!

Were you surprised that Mr. Renkins's buggy won the race? Even though the buggy didn't have a driver, it likely picked up more speed than the other cars because it was bigger and heavier. You can test this theory out with a fun experiment on your next visit to the playground!

**You'll need . . .**
- something to write with
- paper
- balls of different sizes and weights
  (for example: golf ball, tennis ball, baseball, basketball, beach ball)
- a playground slide or other slanted surface
- a way to keep time, such as a stopwatch

**What to do:**
1. Make a list of the balls you gathered. Then make guesses about which ball will roll the fastest and which will be the slowest.
2. One at a time, place each ball at the top of the slide. Start timing as soon as you let go of the ball, and stop timing when the ball rolls off the end of the slide. Record the time next to that ball on your list.

Once you've rolled all your balls down the slide, compare how fast they were. What was the fastest? What was the slowest? How did the results compare to your guesses? Were there any that were almost the same? Why do you think that was?

# What are the parts of a car?

After seeing the pictures in the rulebook, George and Allie made sure they had all of the parts of the boxcar installed before they took to the track. Do you remember what all the parts are called? Check the list below and help George and Allie make sure they have all the right parts by pointing out each part on their boxcar.

**BODY:** The part that a driver sits in.

**AXLE:** The rod that goes through the center of the wheels and allows them to turn.

**STEERING WHEEL:** The wheel connects to the axle to help control the direction of the car.

**WHEELS:** They spin on the axle and allow the car to move.

**BRAKE:** The part that stops the wheels from turning and slows down or stops the car.

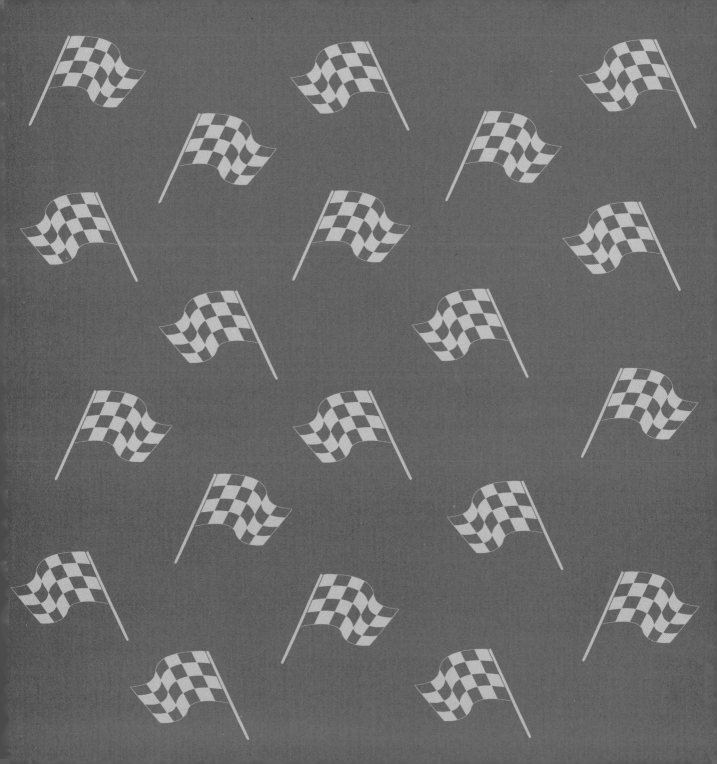

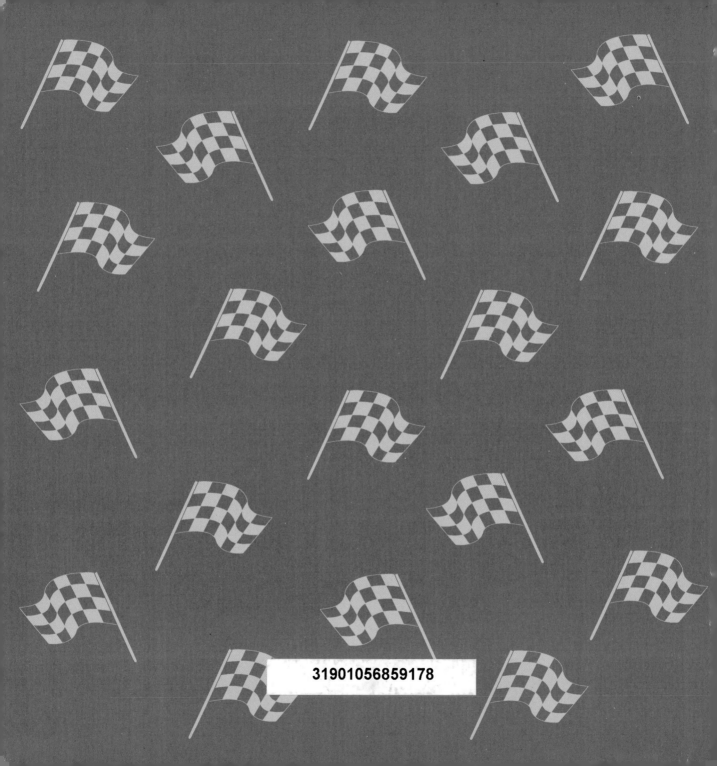